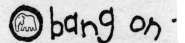 bang on

groovy chick's
diaries

hollywood star

Week

One

Monday am

Fab TV programme about Hollywood.

10 Reasons why Hollywood is cool:

1. Gorgeous Movie Stars
2. Glam Clothes
3. Limousines
4. Pavement Stars
5. Movie Studios
6. Palm Trees
7. Swimming Pools
8. Movie Award Night
9. Hollywood Sign
10. Groovy Weather

4

Great gossip on phone with mates.

i want 2 b a movie star!

It's offical!

Hollywood is our favourite place.

Even my dog thinks so!

People at Hollywood party:

Movie Stars

Fans

Staff

Photographers

Press

Directors

Producers

guests

7

I've got soooo much to do before the Hollywood party.

Get glammed up!

1. Decide what outfit to wear.

2. Buy groovy accessories for outfit.

3. Decide which shoes!

4. Practise movie star hair and make-up styles.

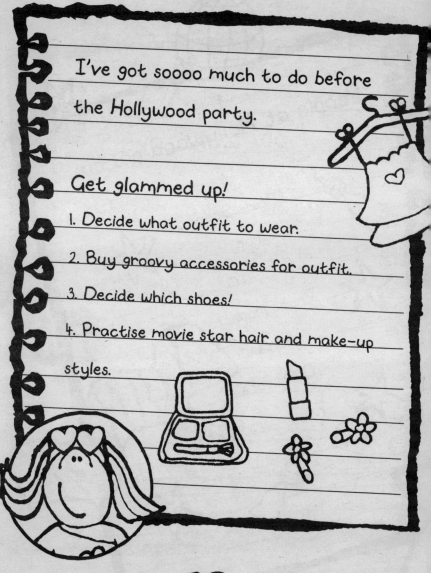

How will I ever

get it all sorted?

I've got exactly

six weeks,

help!

9

7.30am:

Before school:

Check out sparkly items in wardrobe.

8.35am:

Almost late for school!

V. Uncool.

10am:

Eeeek! Almost wore slippers to school! *Blush!*

How embarrassing!

Funky girl 'n' starlet came over and we made guest list for Hollywood party:

funky girl

starlet

drama queen

surf babe

glamour puss

pop princess

me!

Remember to buy feather boa.

11

Friday am

Pop princess, glamour puss, funky girl
and starlet are coming over for a
groovy girly sleepover tonight!

We will need:

Pizza

Sleeping bags

Videos

CDs

Sweets

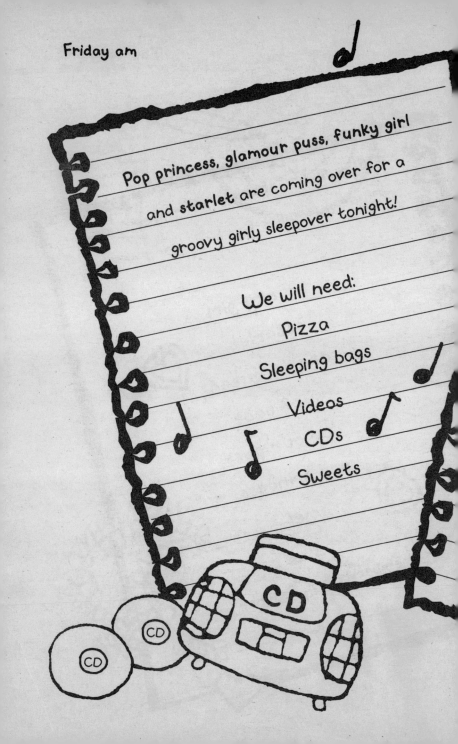

Hanging with your girlfriends is totally wicked! Chatting all night and having lots of laughs! Stayed up really late.

Going shopping for party outfit accessories today. Need:

Bag
Bracelet
Earrings
Lipstick
Feather boa
and lots of glitter!

glitter

14

Pheew!

All that shopping has made me really tired.

Time for a fruity face pack and a soak in the tub with lots of strawberry foam! Look at magazine in bath, lots of pics of movie stars.

So cool!

15

Made totally wicked party invites.

Don't you just love making things?

Let's party!

Two

Put flowers on my desk to help me do my homework! Now my bedroom looks like a star's dressing room (well nearly).

They smell nice too!

Have a Pink Day!

Pink shoes

Hair slides

T-shirt

Pink flowered

Capri pants (nice!)

Wrote in pink all day.

22

Starlet says she's coming to the party totally in fake fur!

Mega glam!

23

Wore fab 'n funky purple outfit.

Sunglasses to match of course!

Glamour puss is sticking sequins

over everything for party.

Sparkly!

glue

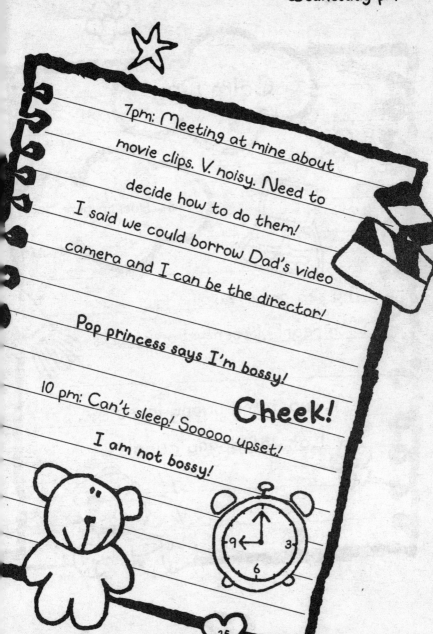

7pm: Meeting at mine about movie clips. V. noisy. Need to decide how to do them!

I said we could borrow Dad's video camera and I can be the director!

Pop princess says I'm bossy!

10 pm: Can't sleep! Sooooo upset!

Cheek!

I am not bossy!

25

Calm Day

Think blue, breathe deep.

Try sea green eyeshadow
with pearl glitter gel on cheeks.

At least my puppy loves me.
Lots of doggy cuddles.

26

Watch sunset

First time all week not mentioned party.

Eeek!

Are my friends going off the party idea?

Soak in calm

lavender bath.

soap

Friday am

Starlet phoned.
She said my movie clip idea is cool.
My Hollywood party will be
a smash hit!
Starlet is my best friend!

Aren't best friends the best?

Go to hobby store for fabulous
jewels to stick on bags,
bracelets, shoes...everything!

glue

Painted
hair mascara
on fringe.
Went a bit blobby!

Dad asked if a pigeon had
flown over me lately!

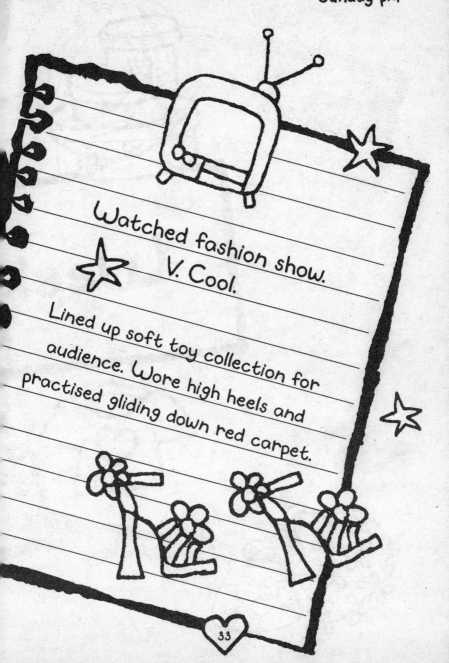

Watched fashion show.
V. Cool.

Lined up soft toy collection for
audience. Wore high heels and
practised gliding down red carpet.

Week

Three

I'm bored with my clothes. What am I going to wear today?

✿ Idea!

1. Sort clothes into piles – t-shirts, skirts, shoes, jeans.

2. Spread piles on bed.

3. Blindfold myself!

4. Pick clothing item from each pile.

Sorted!

I am as stylish as a movie star!

Played Snakes 'n' Ladders with Mum and Dad.

☆ Brill idea! ☆

Decided to invent Hollywood game!

Made up this totally groovy game so we could decide what to wear to the party!

Are you star material?

Are you sometimes moody?

Yes

Always in the spotlight?

Love to be on the cover of a magazine?

Yes

Adore fame?

No

No

Like to sign autographs all day?

Yes

No

No

Dancing

Dancing or sitting?

Yes

Yes

Love to win an award?

No

sitting

Cry if y broke

Yes

Yes

You're a superstar – wear lots of sparkly jewellery to the Hollywood party!

You're a natural-born star – put your hair in a chic style and add some lovely clips!

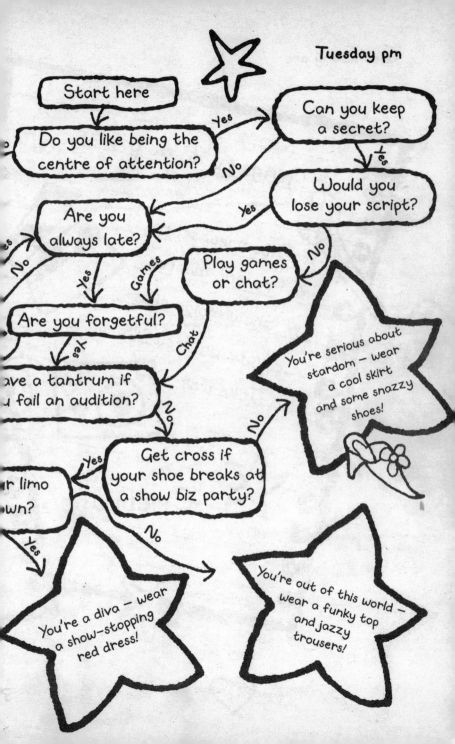

Tuesday pm

Things to do at party:

☆ Interview stars
☆ Present awards
☆ Show movie clips
☆ Vote on best film
☆ Take pics

Celebrate!

40

⭐ Pop princess played guitar
Really groovy. She's a star!

⭐ Pop princess will make
pop video for
Hollywood party!

celebrate!

Hollywood here I come!

HOLLYWOOD

Did maps at school. California is bigger than England! Wow!

Fact: Would-be starlets used to travel miles to Hollywood just to be discovered.

Practised gliding down staircase in high heels with long dress.

Whooooops!

Friday am

Did film poster in Art. V. glam.

Lunchtime:

Practised dance routines in gym.

How cool is that?

Pop princess
upstaged our
dance routine
by singing.

Humph!

Friday pm

Pop princess wants to do
karaoke at my Hollywood party!

No way! This is a movie party!

ven though she's my friend, pop
ncess gets on my nerves sometimes!

45

Saturday am

10am: Go to beach and work on suntan (mustn't forget the sun cream!).

12pm: Meet starlet for lunch and gossip!

3pm: Go through magazines for groovy party hair and make-up ideas!

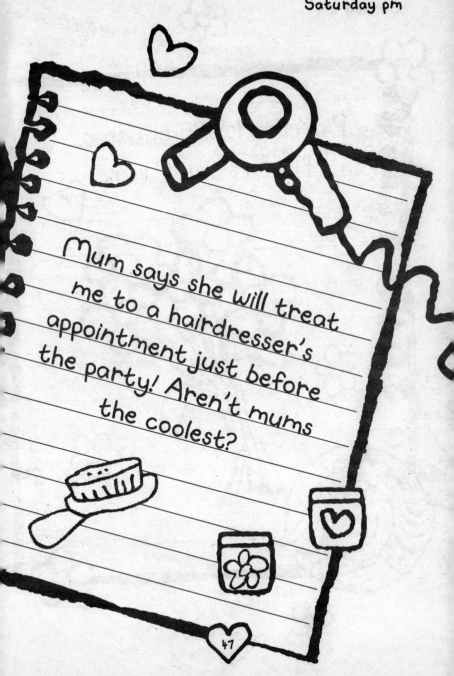

Mum says she will treat me to a hairdresser's appointment just before the party! Aren't mums the coolest?

Picked a lovely bunch of flowers for Mum.

Practised being a movie star,
lazing by the pool
(paddling pool!).

Wore fabulous
bikini with heart
on all day.

Must text friends
about making
movie clips.

49

Wee[k]

The week I

Four

dreamed...

Only two weeks left till the party!

Yikes!

Did handprints in Arts and Crafts. Just like the stars did in the Hollywood walk of fame.

For my fans —

groovy chick

Wore
heart print outfit
to show how much
I love
my fans!

Tuesday am

7.30am: Walk the dog

2.30pm: Had to do interviews in English. I did starlet. Her favourit colour is silver (mine's pink!).

7.30pm: Write up interview for magazine (like Hollywood reporter).

What is your favourite colour?

Text friends:

movies
wed nite?

Stuck flower jewels on toes.
V. pretty.

55

Brill movie!

Dreamed all night
of being a
movie star...

Take make-up round to starlet's tonight.

Don't forget glitter!

glitter

Made a cool beauty
parlour with my friends.
Wicked! **Starlet** is cool.
We will be the most
glam stars ever on
party night.

Practised camera smile

all day.

Carried toy pink poodle

for extra star style.

Mustn't get too

carried away...

Surf babe and me made a groovy soundtrack for Hollywood party.

Cool man!

61

Fashion Ideas:

glue

1. Stick on some sparkly stars.

2. Add chic butterfly patches.

3. Vamp up tired jeans with sequins.

4. Fabric paint fab flowers on t-shirt.

5. Tie dye a groovy scarf.

Dare to be different!

hand dye

salt

62

Made lovely perfume with Mum's flower petals.

Mmmmm...

(It's a girl thing.)

Roller-skating today. Cool!

Went so fast, my poor puppy's legs could hardly keep up!

Wheeeeee!

Roller-skating with your mates is totally fab!

Played ball with my pup.

Week

Hollywoo

starring g

Five

d Party

oouy chick!

Made wicked sign for
Hollywood party.

Hollywood Party Night
starring
groovy chick!

My mates said I was a show-off.

Glamour puss wants to be the biggest star.

So does:

pop princess

surf babe

drama queen

funky girl

But there can only be

One
big star!
Me!

Tuesday am

Acceptance speech for movie award!

I'd like to thank
my mum and dad,
my cute little puppy
and all my mates for
this wonderful award.

Thank you for voting
me the best!

Must not cry!

I'd like to thank
my mum and dad,
my cute little puppy
and all my mates for
this wonderful award.

Thank you for voting
me the BEST!

Tuesday pm

Everyone's telling me to stop showing off and **pop princess** says I'm bossy!

10pm: Can't sleep

I'm soooo upset.

Feeling blue

Wore funky fringe pants
with beaded bag and flip-flops
for a sassy look
(shows I don't care!).

I don't care!

Pop princess is not
speaking to me.

Practised swinging my sunglasses.

Casual or what?

I don't care!

I don't care!

I

...ent to bed early. Boo hoo.

...y my dog loves me.

73

Disaster!

Favourite shoes don't fit!
What will I wear for
the party?

Buried my head
under pillow.

75

Colour co-ordinated my wardrobe.
So busy haven't even noticed that
phone hasn't rung...

76

I know...it must have gone to sleep...

Brill idea!

I'll give my favourite shoes to pop princess. They'll fit her!

Don't fit —

Ran with my lovely puppy.

Yessss!

Made friendship bracelets to put in party gift bags for my friends.

Took a soak in a lovely bubbly bath.

To organise:

decorate party room
(glitter streamers)

popcorr
and car
(make celebrit
nibbles)

red carpet
(spare rug)

Hollywood
(Make from c

spotlights
(ask Dad)

80

silver
screen
(...ake from foil?)

film posters
(draw me and
friends on)

rows of seats
(borrow from
dining table)

...n

limo
(Dad's car)

But will
my friends
come?

Week

Party
Holly

For my fans —

groovy chick

Look!

Dad made groovy silver screen case for TV (my idea) from an old box. Dad rocks!

But who will be the star?

85

Party shopping list

Cheesy snacks

Mini pizzas

Popcorn

Fruit for fancy cocktails

Sparkling drinks

Ice cream

Jelly

On the way to the shops

I met pop princess. She gave

me this letter —

fizz

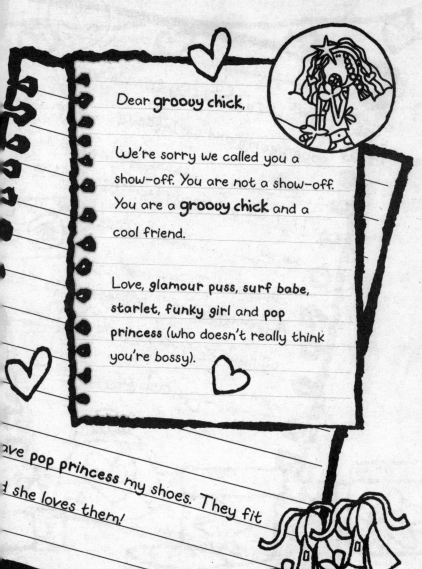

Dear **groovy chick**,

We're sorry we called you a show-off. You are not a show-off. You are a **groovy chick** and a cool friend.

Love, glamour puss, surf babe, starlet, funky girl and pop princess (who doesn't really think you're bossy).

ave pop princess my shoes. They fit

d she loves them!

Party night! My friends came round early and we made up.

Then we got ready together for the party!

A photographer (Dad) took pictures of each star stepping out of her limo. Dead glam!

Each star was interviewed by a TV presenter (Mum) as she made her way past cheering fans, down the red carpet to her seat in the theatre (our living room).

How cool is that?

The stars hardly had time to sign autographs!

My friends went wild over the new names on my new Hollywood party sign. I decided we would *all* be big stars!

✗ Kisses all round!

Waiters (Mum and Dad) came round with trays of sparkly cocktails and cheesy snacks. We watched our groovy film clips.

party!

Lazed around all day eating popcorn and looking at cool pics from our party.

Groovy!

Groovy Chick's Diaries 2:
In The Wild
0-00-717637-6   5/4/2004
The summer holidays are finally here
and **groovy chick's** off to summer camp!
Who will be camp diva and what can she
wear to the disco?
Get out and about and go wild with
your favourite groovy girly.

Groovy Chick's Diaries 3:
Top DJ

0-00-717638-4   6/9/2004

Disco fever gets hold of **groovy chick**
and friends, but being a top DJ is
harder than she realises!
Now you can get into the groove too.
Get ready to disco!

Groovy Chick's Diaries 4:
Circus Crazy

0-00-717641-4   6/9/2004

Swing into action with the one and
only **groovy chick** and friends!
Groovy chick goes circus crazy, but can
she master her big top skills in time
to amaze everyone?

First published in Great Britain by
HarperCollins Children's Books in 2004

1 3 5 7 9 10 8 6 4 2

ISBN: 0 00 717636 8

A CIP catalogue record for this title is available
from the British Library.

The HarperCollins website address is:
www.harpercollinschildrensbooks.co.uk

Printed and bound in the UK
by Bookmarque Ltd.